DOG BRAIN

By David Milgrim

D0580536

VIKING

VIKING   Published by the Penguin Group
Penguin Books USA Inc., 375 Hudson Street, New York, New York 10014, U.S.A.
Penguin Books Ltd, 27 Wrights Lane, London W8 5TZ, England
Penguin Books Australia Ltd, Ringwood, Victoria, Australia
Penguin Books Canada Ltd, 10 Alcorn Avenue, Toronto, Ontario, Canada M4V 3B2
Penguin Books (N.Z.) Ltd, 182–190 Wairau Road, Auckland 10, New Zealand

Penguin Books Ltd, Registered Offices: Harmondsworth, Middlesex, England

First published in 1996 by Viking, a division of Penguin Books USA Inc.

10 9 8 7 6 5 4 3 2 1

LIBRARY OF CONGRESS CATALOGING-IN-PUBLICATION DATA
Milgrim, David.   Dog brain / by David Milgrim.   p. cm.
Summary: A young boy figures his dog Sneakers must be really smart to act so dumb.
ISBN 0-670-86935-X
[1. Dogs—Fiction. 2. Behavior—Fiction.] I. Title.
PZ7.M5955Do 1996 [E]—dc20   95-50539 CIP AC

Set in Magna Carta

The artwork was done in black ink and gouache.

Reprinted by arrangement with Penguin Putnam Inc.
Printed in the USA.

For Gogo, Kyra + Pop

My dog Sneakers
acts dumb,
but I think
he's faking it.

But my mom and dad
are totally fooled.

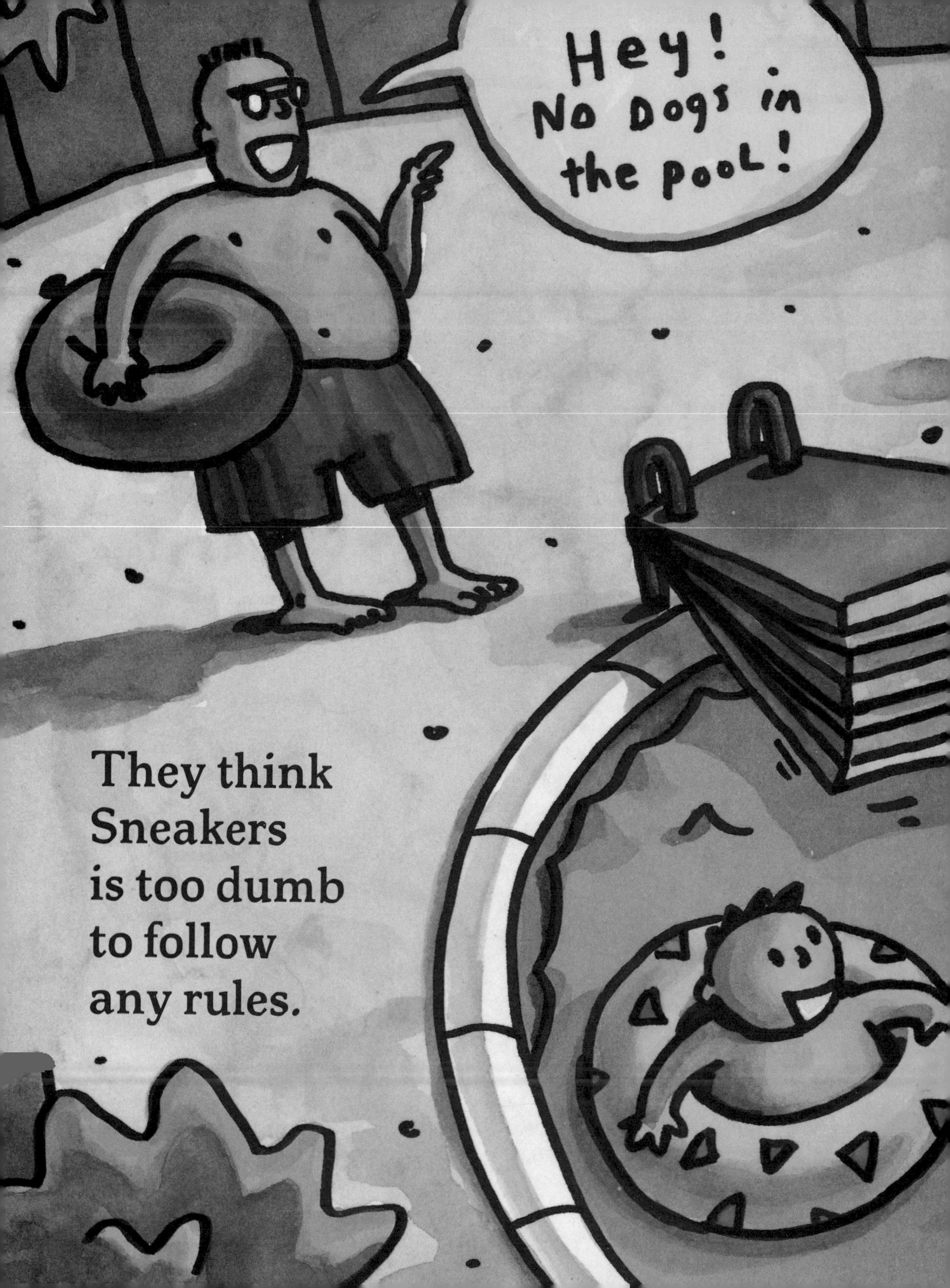

They think
Sneakers
is too dumb
to follow
any rules.

Or to listen to
anything he's told.

They think Sneakers
is too dumb to behave
himself at all.

But I don't buy it
for a second.

In fact, I wouldn't be
surprised if Sneakers
slips out at night
after we're asleep.

And meets his friends
for coffee and fries.

And goes to wild, all-night beach parties.

And sees movies about dogs, made by dogs, with dog actors, in secret, all-dog movie theaters where after the show everyone agrees to act dumb.

Nope,
it wouldn't
surprise me
one bit.

Sometimes I wonder if Sneakers will ever tell us his secret. But I guess that wouldn't be very smart.

And so on he goes . . .
But he doesn't fool me.

I know a genius
when I see one.